# ATTENTION, BÊTES FÉROCES !

Pour Tristan, Rhys et Stefan

Texte français de Claude Lager

Loi 49956 du 16 juillet 1949,
sur les publications destinées à la jeunesse.
Dépôt légal : septembre 2009
ISBN 978-2-211-09573-0

Typographie : Architexte, Bruxelles
Imprimé et relié à Singapour

# ATTENTION, BÊTES FÉROCES !

## Chris Wormell

Pastel

*l'école des loisirs*

Un ours flânait dans la forêt…

quand il rencontra un petit garçon
assis sur une souche.
Il avait l'air triste.

«Que se passe-t-il ?» demanda l'ours.
«Je me suis perdu, dit l'enfant en reniflant. C'est terrible !»
«Et pourquoi ça ?»
«Parce que ma maman m'a interdit de me promener
dans la forêt. J'ai désobéi et maintenant, je suis perdu !»

«Ne t'en fais pas, dit l'ours en souriant,
je vais t'aider à retrouver ton chemin.
La forêt n'est pas si dangereuse que ça, tu sais.»
«Oh si ! affirma l'enfant. Ma maman a dit
que la forêt est remplie de bêtes féroces !»

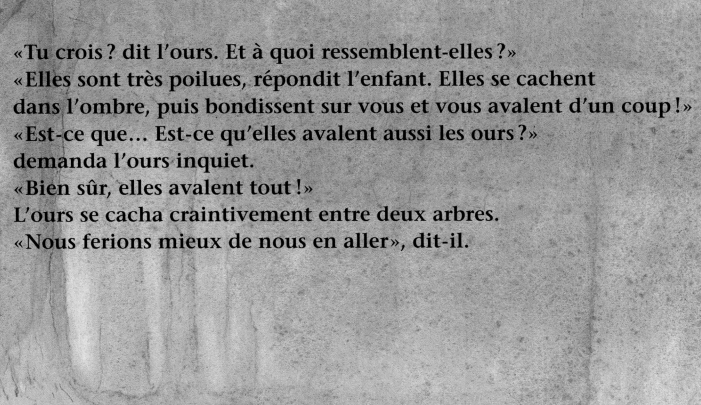

«Tu crois ? dit l'ours. Et à quoi ressemblent-elles ?»
«Elles sont très poilues, répondit l'enfant. Elles se cachent
dans l'ombre, puis bondissent sur vous et vous avalent d'un coup !»
«Est-ce que… Est-ce qu'elles avalent aussi les ours ?»
demanda l'ours inquiet.
«Bien sûr, elles avalent tout !»
L'ours se cacha craintivement entre deux arbres.
«Nous ferions mieux de nous en aller», dit-il.

Un peu plus loin,
ils rencontrèrent un éléphant qui cassait la croûte.
«Quelqu'un veut une banane?» demanda l'éléphant.

«Tu ferais mieux de prendre garde, Éléphant, fit l'ours.
Ce jeune homme me dit qu'il y a des bêtes féroces qui rôdent !»
«Mince ! dit l'éléphant en lâchant sa banane.
Elles sont si féroces que ça ?»

«Les plus féroces du monde, dit le garçon. Elles sont tellement énormes qu'elles peuvent t'écraser et te réduire en bouillie. Comme ça!»

«Mais… tu ne crois quand même pas qu'elles peuvent écraser un éléphant?» demanda l'éléphant.

«Bien sûr que si!» répondit le garçon.

«Oh ! purée ! s'étrangla l'éléphant.
Ça ne vous dérange pas si je fais un bout de chemin avec vous ?»

Tous trois marchèrent prudemment dans la forêt.
Bientôt, ils rencontrèrent un lion qui prenait un bain de soleil
sur un rocher. «Installez-vous et profitez du soleil», dit le lion
en agitant la queue.

«Sûrement pas, répondit l'ours.
Ignores-tu qu'il y a des bêtes féroces dans les environs ?»
Le lion sursauta.
«Hein ! Des bêtes féroces ? Vraiment féroces ?»

«Les plus féroces qui existent, déclara le garçon. Elles ont des griffes acérées et de grandes dents capables de vous arracher la tête en une seconde !»

«Quoi ! rugit le lion. Elles ne peuvent pas faire ça à un lion, tout de même ?»

«Je crois bien que le lion est
leur plat préféré», dit le garçon.
«Au secours! hurla le lion,
la crinière toute hérissée.
Dites, ça ne vous ennuie pas
si je vous accompagne?»

Sur la pointe des pattes,
ils continuèrent à cheminer dans la forêt.
Ils rencontrèrent bientôt un crocodile...
Puis un loup... Puis un python.

Le soleil avait presque disparu.
«C'est à la tombée de la nuit que les bêtes féroces
sortent pour chasser», dit le garçon.

Juste à ce moment-là, un bruit terrible
retentit... comme si un animal monstrueux
pénétrait dans le sous-bois.

Une lumière se mit à clignoter entre les troncs d'arbre:
on aurait dit qu'un œil phosphorescent les observait…

C'est alors qu'un hurlement sauvage résonna dans la forêt…

# Sauve qui peut !

Tous s'enfuirent. Tous, excepté le petit garçon,
qui était le plus courageux. Il s'avança prudemment
et constata que ce n'était pas du tout une bête féroce.
C'était bien pire que ça…

C'était
sa féroce
**maman !**

«Antoine ! Antoine ! rugit-elle.
Où es-tu, vilain garçon ?»

«Oh ! tu es là ! soupira-t-elle. Je t'avais pourtant bien dit de ne **jamais** aller dans la forêt ! Je t'avais pourtant bien dit que plein de bêtes féroces vivent ici !»

«Mais Maman, protesta Antoine,
je n'ai vu aucune bête féroce!»

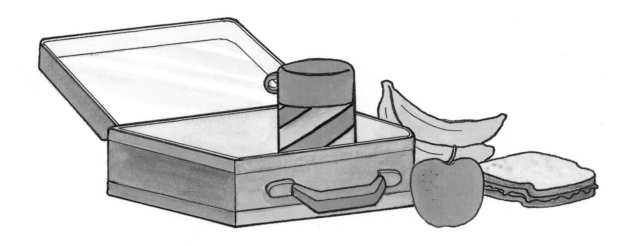

To women of words,
a fantastic bunch of kids — WOW!

SGT & JRE

To my father

M.A.F.

A Preschool **Read·A·Picture** Book™

# Little Kids at School

Written by Jeffie Ross Gordon
Illustrated by Mary Ann Fraser

**MODERN PUBLISHING**
A Division of Unisystems, Inc.
New York, NY 10022

# Table of Contents

# Ethan's First Day of School

# Words for Ethan's First Day of School

 Ethan

 book

 Emmy

 teddy bear

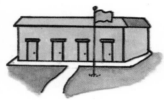 school

 four

 lunch box

# Ethan's First Day of School

"Today is your first day at Rainbow 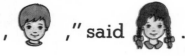, ," said .

"I have my blue . I have my red . But I don't have my ," said .

"Your  cannot go to , ," said .

"But my  is my friend," said . "I will not have a friend at ."

"You will have lots of friends at ," said .

"Who will be my friend?" asked .

"There are Scott and Jane," said .

"They are my friends," said .

"And I am your friend. Your teacher is your friend, too," said .

"Hurray!" said . "Now I have **4** friends at 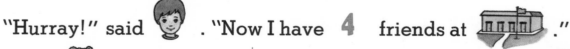."

"Your  will wait for you at home until you return from ," said 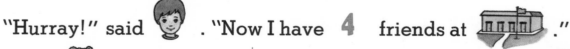.

# Clay Time

# New words for Clay Time

 table

 duck

 ball

 Pooch

 frog

 cow

 pig

# Words you have learned

 Emmy

 school

# Clay Time

It was clay time at Rainbow  .

 and Jane sat at the clay  .

 rolled her clay into a  . "I am making a  ," said  .

"It does not look like a  ," said Jane.

 rolled her clay into a big  . "This is a  ," said  .

"It does not look like a  ," said Jane.

 rolled her clay into a bigger  . "I am making  ," said

 .

"It does not look like  ," said Jane.

Then  rolled her clay into a much bigger  .

"Are you making a big  ?" asked Jane.

"No," said  .

"Are you making a big  ?" asked Jane.

"No," said .

"What are you making?" asked Jane.

"I am making a big ," said .

15

# A New Friend

# New words for A New Friend

 apple

## Words you have learned

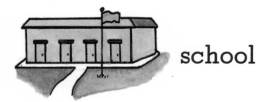 school

 Emmy

 book

 ball

# A New Friend

A new girl, Nancy, came to Rainbow  .

"Do you want to look at our ?" asked  and Jane.

"Yes," said Nancy.

 and Jane and Nancy looked at the  .

"Would you like to share our  ?" asked  and Jane.

"Yes, please," said Nancy.

 and Jane and Nancy shared the  .

"Let's play with our  ," said  and Jane.

"Okay," said Nancy.

 and Jane and Nancy played with the  .

"Do you want to be my new friends?" asked Nancy.

"You bet," said  and Jane.

Nancy and  and Jane are all new friends.

# The New Teacher

Scott

Rachel

# New words for The New Teacher

 bed

 tree

 dinosaur

 bird

# Words you have learned

 Ethan

 teddy bear

 school

# The New Teacher

 and Scott were at Rainbow  .

"I am Mr. Brown," said the man to the class. "I am your teacher for the day."

"Where is Mrs. Green?" asked  .

"Mrs. Green is home sick in  ," said Mr. Brown.

"Does she have the chicken pox?" asked  . "I was sick in  with the chicken pox."

"No. Mrs. Green has a cold. She will be back soon," said Mr. Brown.

"Today, we will draw get-well pictures for Mrs. Green. The pictures will make her feel better."

Scott drew a  . He also drew a  and a  .

"That is a very nice get-well picture of a  ," said Mr. Brown. "What did you draw,  ?"

"I drew my  ," said  . "He made me feel better when I had the chicken pox."

Your  is a perfect get-well picture," said Mr. Brown.

# Three Stars for Emmy

# New words for Three Stars for Emmy

 star

 crayons

 doll

**1** one

**2** two

**3** three

## Words you have learned

 Emmy

 school

# Three Stars for Emmy

 wanted a  on her Rainbow  chart.

"Take out your  ," said Mrs. Gray.

"I lost my red and blue  ," said Jane.

"You may share mine," said  .

"Thank you," said Jane.

 and Jane colored together.

"Time for show and tell," said Mrs. Gray.

"I forgot my  ," said Jane.

"Share my  ," said  . "You show her and I will tell about the  ."

"Thank you," said Jane.

"Now it is  time," said Mrs. Gray. "Jane gets **1**  for coloring

and **1**  for show and tell.

"That makes **2** ," said Jane.

"I'm glad you got **2** ," said  .

"Today,  gets **1**  for coloring and **1**  for show and tell.

She gets a special  for sharing," said Mrs. Gray.

"Thank you," said  . "Now I have **3** ."

# Animal Sounds

# New words for Animal Sounds

 rooster

 toaster

# Words you have learned

 pig

 duck

 cow

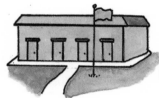 school

 Ethan

# Animal Sounds

It was time to play at Rainbow  .

"Let's play animal sounds," said  .

"I will be a  ," said  . "Cock-a-doodle-doo!"

"I will be a  ," said Scott. "Quack-a-doodle-doo!"

"I will be a  ," said  . "Oink-a-doodle-doo!"

"I will be a  ," said Scott. "Moo-a-doodle-doo!"

"I will be a  ," said  .

"A toaster doesn't say anything," said Scott.

"Yes, it does," said  . "A  says pop-a-doodle-doo!"

# Trading Lunches

# New words for Trading Lunches

 sandwich

 cookies

**10** ten

 cake

 cherries

**5** five

# Words you have learned

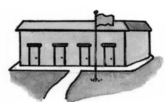 school

**2** two

 Emmy

**1** one

 apple

 lunch box

# Trading Lunches

It was lunch time at Rainbow .

Jane had a peanut butter and jelly . She had an  and **1** piece of .

 had a peanut butter and honey . She had **10**  and **2** .

"I like peanut butter and jelly," said . "I like an  and , too."

"I like peanut butter and honey," said Jane. "I like  and , too."

"Let's share," said .

Jane gave  half of her . She gave her half of her  and a piece of her .

 gave Jane half of her . She gave her **5**  and **1** of her .

"Now our lunches are the same," said Jane.

"No they are not," said . "My  is blue. Your  is red."

Jane laughed.

Aa Bb Cc Dd Ee Ff Gg Hh Ii Jj Kk Ll Mm

# Story Time

# New words for Storytime

 ducks

 bunnies

 frogs

 dogs

# Words you have learned

 Ethan

 book

# Story Time

"Story time," said Mrs. Green .

"Hurray!", shouted 🧒 .

"Hurray," said Scott.

"Please read a 📖 about 🐤 ," said 🧒 . "I like stories about 🐤 ."

"Please read a 📖 about 🐸 ," said Scott. "I like stories about 🐸 ."

"And a 📖 about 🐰 ," said 🧒 . "I like stories about 🐰 ."

"And a 📖 about 🐶 ," said Scott. "I like stories about 🐶 ."

"A 📖 about 🐤 and 🐸 and 🐰 and 🐶 ," said Mrs. Green. "I think I will read a 📖 of poems, today."

"Hurray!" said 🧒 . "Please read poems about 🐤 and 🐸 and 🐰 and 🐶 ."

39

# The Sandbox

# New words for The Sandbox

 sandbox

 dog

 pond

 bunny

# Words you have learned

 Ethan

 frog

 duck

 Emmy

# The Sandbox

"Race you to the 🟫 , Scott," said 👦 .

Scott and 👦 ran fast.

Scott won.

"We can play in the 🟫 ," said 👦 . "The 🟫 will be our 🌿 ."

"I do not want to be a 🦆 ," said Scott. "I will be a 🐸 ."

"Then I will be a 🦆 ," said 👦 . "You will be the 🐸 ."

👧 and Jane came to play in the 🟫 .

"I want to be a 🐰 ," said 👧 . "I want to play in the 🟫 , too."

"I want to be a 🐶 and play in the 🟫 ," said Jane.

"This is not a 🟫 ," said 👦 . "This is a 🌿 ."

"A 🐰 and a 🐶 cannot play in a 🌿 ," said Scott.

"This 🌿 is full of sand," said 👧 .

"Make room for a 🐰 and a 🐶 in the sand 🌿 ," said Jane.

43

# Words You Have Learned in Little Kids at School

| | |
|---|---|
| Ethan | four |
| Emmy | table |
| school | ball |
| lunch box | frog |
| book | pig |
| teddy bear | duck |
| | Pooch |
| | cow |
| | apple |
| | bed |
| | dinosaur |
| | tree |
| | bird |

star

crayons

doll

one

two

three

rooster

toaster

sandwich

ten

cherries

cookies

cake

five

ducks

frogs

bunnies

dogs

sandbox

pond

dog

bunny

1

2